BERNADETTE WATTS has illustrated many classic fairy tales for NorthSouth, including *The Bremen Town Musicians, The Snow Queen,* and *The Ugly Duckling.* Bernadette Watts lives in England.

NorthSouth

First published in the United States, Great Britain, Canada, Australia, and New Zealand in
2000 by NorthSouth Books Inc., an imprint of NordSüd Verlag AG, CH-8005 Zürich, Switzerland.

First paperback edition published in 2007 by NorthSouth Books Inc.
Distributed in the United States by North-South Books Inc., New York 10016.

Library of Congress Cataloging-in-Publication Data is available.
A CIP catalogue record for this book is available from The British Library.

ISBN-13: 978-0-7358-1220-8 / ISBN-10: 0-7358-1220-9 (trade edition)
10 9 8 7 6 5 4 3 2
ISBN 978-0-7358-2129-3 (paperback edition)
10 9 8 7 6 5 4 3

Printed in China by Toppan Leefung Packaging & Printing (Dongguan) Co., Ltd.,
Dongguan, P.R.C., July 2012

FSC
www.fsc.org
MIX
Paper from
responsible sources
FSC® C104723

The Lion and the Mouse

A FABLE BY AESOP RETOLD
AND ILLUSTRATED BY

Bernadette Watts

NorthSouth
New York / London

The lion cubs played happily in the sunshine while their parents slept nearby. The day grew hotter and hotter, so hot that the cubs grew tired. One by one they lay down to rest in the shade near their parents. Only one of the cubs kept on playing despite the heat.

When the blazing sun was at its highest, however, it was too hot even for him, so he padded over to a shady spot at the edge of the jungle and went to sleep.

Suddenly, a little mouse scampered across the sleeping lion cub's paw, tickling him and waking him up. The lion cub snarled angrily.

The mouse froze—too terrified to run away. "I'm sorry I woke you," she said, trembling.

When the lion saw that it was only a harmless little mouse, he smiled and said, "Off you go, little one. I won't hurt you."

"Oh, thank you for sparing my life!" said the mouse. "One day I will repay your kindness. If you ever need help, send for me."

The lion laughed out loud. "I am much bigger and stronger than you!" he said. "And soon I shall be even bigger and stronger. A mouse cannot help a lion."

Then the lion stood up and stretched to show just how big and strong he was. Proudly, he walked away.

The mouse ran in the other direction.

Years passed, and the cub grew into
the biggest and strongest of all the lions.
He was now the king of the beasts.

The days were long and hot, and every day at
noon the great lion would go to sleep in the shade.
If the mouse happened to run by, she kept well
away from the lion's paws.

One day when the lion headed for his resting spot, he fell into a trap! The more he struggled to get free, the more he entangled himself in the net.

The king of the beasts was caught! He gave a mighty roar. He roared with rage. He roared in fear. Then he roared for help.

The animals of the day heard his call and rushed up to him. But they couldn't help.

Night fell, and the lion was still trapped in the net.
The animals of the night crept up to see the captured
lion. But they couldn't help him either.

Early the next morning, the mouse appeared.
"You called for me?" she asked. "I will help you,
as I promised I would years ago."

The lion looked at the mouse in amazement.
"No one can help me," he said. "Least of all you."

The mouse started nibbling through the cords of
the net, one after another. "Be patient, Lion," she
said. "Soon you will be free."

Before long the mouse had chewed a hole in the
net, and the lion pushed himself through it.

The lion was free! He stood before the mouse and bowed his head. "Thank you, little mouse," he said. "I will never again laugh at someone weaker or smaller than myself. To repay your kindness, I promise I will always protect you."

And so the lion and the mouse remained the best of friends until the end of their days.